Disney Adventures

CASEBUSTERS

11

The Internet Escapade

Disney Adventures

11

CASEBUSTERS

The Internet Escapade

By Joan Lowery Nixon

New York

With love to the Brush family:
Kathy, Kirk, Melia, Nicole, and Veronica.
Special thanks to Dwight Silverman,
the *Houston Chronicle*'s technology writer,
for his helpful advice.

—J. L. N.

 For information, address Disney Press, 114 Fifth Avenue, New York, NY 10011-5690.

Printed in the United States of America.
First edition

1 3 5 7 9 10 8 6 4 2

Library of Congress Catalog Card Number: 96-70875

ISBN: 0-7868-4088-9

Adventures in the CASEBUSTERS series:

The Statue Walks at Night
The Legend of Deadman's Mine
Backstage with a Ghost
Check in to Danger
The House Has Eyes
Secret of the Time Capsule
Beware the Pirate Ghost
Catch a Crooked Clown
Fear Stalks Grizzly Hill
Sabotage on the Set

1

"LOOK OUT! DEBBIE JEAN'S coming this way!" Sean Quinn nudged his friend Matt Fischer, who quickly turned the knob that darkened their computer screen.

Sean pretended that he hadn't seen Debbie Jean. But from the corner of his eye he carefully watched her walk through Redoaks Elementary School's media center. Bossy Debbie Jean Parker was a real pain. Sean hated the way she always tried to find out what everybody else in class was doing so she could tell them how to do it. Sean held his breath as she came close. Would she . . . would she . . . ?

As Debbie Jean pulled out a chair and sat in front of her favorite computer, Matt let out a snicker.

Sean poked him. "Don't make her suspicious," Sean whispered, but he wanted to laugh so badly he could hardly stand it.

Matt lightened up the computer screen again and began to type.

Debbie Jean scowled and muttered, "Something's wrong with this computer."

Sean clapped his hands over his mouth, but a small laugh burst out. Quickly, he turned and pretended to be reading the poster on the wall behind him. He was sure that Debbie Jean was looking at him.

As Matt kept typing, Debbie Jean leaned closer to the screen of her computer and stared at the words on it.

She began typing something on her

keyboard, then stopped and frowned again. Sean's stomach hurt, he wanted to laugh so much.

Debbie Jean grabbed the mouse and shook it. "This stupid computer is broken!" she cried. Jumping up, she knocked her chair over.

As she picked it up, she glanced at Matt and Sean, who quickly pretended to be reading something on their monitor. They waited until Debbie Jean stomped out of sight, then they broke down laughing.

"That was great," Matt said. "We really fooled her."

"What did you type?" Sean asked.

Matt grinned. "I wrote, I'M A MAGIC COMPUTER. I'M GOING TO TURN YOU INTO A ROBOT, AND YOU'LL HAVE TO DO WHATEVER I SAY. Then she wrote back, THAT'S WHAT YOU THINK."

"She sure looked angry," Sean said. "This is a great trick."

"Yeah," Matt said. "I'm glad that Dennis Taylor told us how to do it."

Sean ran over to the computer Debbie Jean had used, cleared the screen, then hurried back to Matt. "Shhh!" Sean whispered. "Someone's coming."

Charlie, Sam Miyako's little brother, came into the media center and sat at the computer Debbie had just left.

Matt began typing on his computer keyboard, but Sean said, "Let him alone. He's not only our next-door neighbor, he's just a little kid. Besides, Charlie gets spooked real easy. Sam's always telling him scary stories."

Charlie leaned forward to read the message on his screen and gasped.

"What did you write to him?" Sean asked.

"I wrote him, I'M A MAGIC COMPUTER, AND YOU GET THREE WISHES," Matt whispered.

Charlie began to type with one finger, carefully hitting one letter at a time. The message slowly came up on the screen in front of Sean and Matt.

I WISH FOR A GIANT CANDY BAR, A NEW BIKE, AND A MONSTER UNDER MY BROTHER'S BED.

"Cool," Matt said. "I'd like to see that monster, too."

Sean felt a pang of guilt. "Charlie's going to be disappointed when he doesn't get his wishes."

"Hey," Matt said. "It's only a game. Okay?"

Sean was intent on watching what Charlie continued to write: I NEVER MET A MAGIC COMPUTER . . . He jumped when a stern voice behind them said, "Sean! Matt! Turn around please."

Mrs. Harrison, the school's media specialist, stared down at them. "We had a complaint about one of the computers, and now I see why. Isn't it amazing how your hands are off the keyboard, yet letters continue to appear on your screen?"

Sean could feel his face burn as Mrs. Harrison asked, "You crossed the wires, didn't you?"

"Uh, yeah. We were kind of playing a trick," Sean tried to explain. "We connected the monitor where Charlie's sitting with this keyboard, and vice versa." He couldn't help smiling a little when he remembered how confused know-it-all Debbie Jean had looked.

Mrs. Harrison didn't smile back. "I certainly don't have to ask where you came up with this idea," she said crossly. "Ever since the students from the junior high computer club began coming here as volunteers, you two have tried every computer trick the older students brag about. Well, this time you both go straight to the principal's office. We'll see what Mr. Burns has to say about this."

"Yes, Mrs. Harrison," Sean answered. He felt sick in the pit of his stomach. The trick had been so much fun that he hadn't thought about what might happen if he and Matt were caught. He looked at Matt. Matt looked as if he didn't feel very well either.

What was Mr. Burns going to do?

2

SEAN AND MATT squirmed in the two large visitors' chairs in the principal's office, while Mr. Burns stared down at them from his height of six feet, two inches. Straining to look up that far made Sean's neck ache. Mr. Burns was usually a smiling, friendly principal, but at the moment he wasn't smiling and he didn't seem very friendly.

"Just because there are pranksters in the junior high's computer club, it doesn't mean you have to copy them," Mr. Burns said. "Mrs. Harrison was quite upset last week when you played—what was it—oh, yes, Color Nuts on the computers."

"That program didn't hurt anybody," Matt said. "It just kept changing the monitors' background colors every few seconds."

Mr. Burns didn't smile. He frowned at Sean and Matt. "How about when you set up a computer to read, 'for more information press control, alt, delete'? What's funny about that?"

"Uh, we thought it was funny when some of the kids from the computer club did it," Matt answered.

"Unfortunately, our Redoaks Elementary students working on the computers didn't think so, since the command turned off their computers and they lost all their work," Mr. Burns said. "I hope you give some thought to the students you tricked today and either apologize or make it up to them by some act of kindness. I'll give you a few days. Then I'll expect you to report that the matter has been taken care of."

As Matt and Sean left the office, Sean made a face. "I can't apologize to Debbie Jean. It will make me barf." He suddenly stopped complaining and began to smile. "'Course, if she happens to get in the way . . ."

The bell rang, and a door flew open. Sean and Matt had to jump out of the path of a trampling herd of first graders.

Charlie careened into Sean and tugged at his sleeve. His eyes shining, Charlie said, "Sean! Guess what? I got the magic computer!"

"Charlie, there isn't—" Sean began, but Charlie interrupted.

"Yes, there is, and it gave me three wishes. They're secret, so don't ask what they are because I can't tell you or they won't come true."

As Charlie ran to catch up with his class, he shouted back over his shoulder, "But I can tell everybody I'm going to get my wishes!"

"What are we going to do about making it up to Charlie?" Sean asked.

"What Mr. Burns said. Tell Charlie what we did and apologize."

"We can't do that," Sean said. "Didn't you see how excited he was?" He thought a moment, then said, "Since he lives next door to me, it'll be easy to make his first wish come true. I'll get a big candy bar and hide it on his pillow, under the bedspread."

Matt frowned. "A candy bar's no problem. But where are we going to come up with enough money to get him his second wish—a new bike?"

"Uh, yeah. We'll have to think about it, and about the monster, too." Sean groaned.

"I know where we can get a monster," Matt said. "We could buy a big ugly squid at the fish market and put it under Sam's bed!"

Sean chuckled, but he said, "It won't work. Think how the squid would stink. Mrs. Miyako would be mad at us for the next hundred years, and she'd call our mothers, and—"

"Okay. No squid," Matt agreed.

During the last hour of school and all the way home, Sean tried to think of some way to fill Charlie's order for a bicycle, but he couldn't come up with a single good idea. However, as Sean entered the kitchen and flopped into a seat at the table, he saw that a package had arrived. It was from Grandma, who was on a spring cruise in Alaska. And the package had his and his brother's names on the label.

Immediately feeling better, Sean tore open the box and ripped the paper off his package.

He laughed as he pulled out a pair of bedroom slippers that were designed to look like huge, fuzzy bear paws, complete with yellow, curved claws.

"Cool!" Sean said.

Sean's brother, Brian, didn't get home from school until just a few minutes before Mrs. Quinn arrived home from her job at the advertising agency. Brian laughed at Sean's slippers and admired the hand-carved totem-pole key chain Grandma had sent him. But his mind was on something more important.

"I've got some really great news," Brian said. "I won the Top Student of the Month award at school." Out of his backpack he pulled a certificate signed by the Redoaks Junior High principal and a fistful of coupons, which he tossed on the table.

Mrs. Quinn hugged Brian, saying, "Oh,

Brian, I'm so proud of you! What a wonderful award!"

But Sean took one look at the coupons and yelled, "Bri, free ice cream and a free hamburger! And look! You've got free coupons for Monstermadness!

"Two of them," Brian said. "How about coming with me?"

"Wow!" Sean said. "When?"

"How about Friday?"

"Sure. That's great." With a rush of gratitude toward his big brother, Sean added, "It's real cool of you to share them with me."

Brian turned to Mrs. Quinn. "I wish Dad wasn't away on a business trip so I could tell him my news," he said.

Mrs. Quinn smiled and hugged Brian again. "Why don't you telephone him tonight?" she asked.

She reached out another arm for Sean and drew him close. “How about you, Sean? Do you have any good news for your dad?”

Sean’s stomach felt weird again. He took a deep breath and answered, “Well . . . um . . . nothing special. I’ll just say hello to Dad. That’s all.”

While Brian tackled homework and Mrs. Quinn cooked dinner, Sean decided to use his dad’s computer to play one of the games. To his surprise he found an E-mail message addressed to Sean Quinn: YOU GOT YOURSELF IN TROUBLE TODAY. YOU HAD TO GO TO THE PRINCIPAL’S OFFICE. YOU AND MATT WON’T BE THE ONLY ONES IN TROUBLE FOR LONG. TOMORROW MR. BURNS IS GOING TO HAVE PROBLEMS OF HIS OWN.

“Uh-oh,” Sean whispered. He looked to both sides, as if whoever wrote the E-mail was staring at him. How did this person know that I went to Mr. Burns's office? Sean wondered. What does it mean about the principal having problems? And what does that have to do with me?

Creepy!

3

SEAN RAN UP to Brian's bedroom and said, "C'mon, quick! There's something on the computer you have to see!"

Brian trotted down the stairs after Sean and followed him to the computer. Brian took one look and said, "E-mail? To you?"

"Read it," Sean said.

Brian did, then turned to Sean. "What kind of trouble did you get into?"

"Not so loud," Sean said nervously. "Mom might hear."

Brian lowered his voice, but he said, "How can I help you, if I don't know what's going on?"

"Okay," Sean said. "Remember when Dennis Taylor told us how he switched the hookup on two computers, so what people wrote ended up on each other's screens? Well, that's what Matt and I did, only some people don't have a very good sense of humor and we got sent to Mr. Burns's office. Someone who knows about it wrote this E-mail letter, but I don't know who it's from."

"It's easy to find out," Brian said. "We'll check the sender's E-mail return address." He leaned toward the screen and then stopped. "Hey!" he said. "That's weird. The log-in name and address are missing. This is an anonymous mailer, so there's no record of who sent the message."

Sean peered at the screen. "Maybe it's from Matt. He loves to play tricks with his computer."

"Didn't you tell me once that Matt had an account at your school?"

"Yeah, he does."

"Okay then. It can't be from Matt or from any other kids at Redoaks," Brian explained. "Because on the school accounts no one would be able to write a mailer without identification."

"I don't get it," Sean said. "The computer always shows an Internet I.D. for anyone writing an E-mail letter. I don't understand how someone can send an anonymous mailer."

"It's easy enough, if you know the right connections," Brian told him. "On the Internet there are a series of computers known as anonymous remailers. You send mail to a remailer computer. It strips your name off your message, then forwards it to the person you want it to go to. You couldn't do it from school, though; you'd get caught."

"Does everybody know about these remailers?" Sean asked.

"No, but they're not hard to find," Brian answered. "The kids who are really into computers know about them."

"Like Dennis?"

Brian shrugged. "Sure. He's the one who told me about remailers."

Sean thought a moment and said, "I think whoever wrote to me is somebody from my school. Who else would know about Mr. Burns and about my getting into trouble and having to go to the office?"

Sean glanced over his shoulder, as if someone were standing in the shadows of the den, spying on him. But no one was there.

THE NEXT MORNING, as Sean plopped his books on top of his classroom desk, Debbie Jean faced him with a smirk. "Your computer mix-up was a dumb joke," she said. "When you pull anything that stupid, you deserve to get caught."

"It was worth it," Sean said, "to see you arguing with your computer and yelling that it was broken."

Some of the kids giggled, and Sean smiled. Debbie Jean's face turned red, but she said, "You didn't fool me for a minute. Besides, I—"

The bell rang, and Mrs. Jackson said, "Settle

down, class. Let's all stop talking and sit down quietly."

Sean sighed with relief that he didn't have to hear any more of Debbie Jean's complaints, but his relief didn't last long. The intercom crackled, and a stern voice boomed into the room: "Sean Quinn and Matt Fischer, please report to the principal's office."

Matt was at the dentist, so Sean realized that he'd have to face this problem alone. He climbed out of his desk and started toward the nearest door.

Larry Grier leaned out of his desk and snickered as Sean passed him. "Sean's in trouble again," Larry said loudly. "What did you do this time, Sean?"

No one had to tell Sean that he must be in some kind of trouble. But what? Sean wondered if being ordered to go to the principal's office had something to do with the anonymous E-mail he'd received the day before.

He got the answer the moment he entered Mr. Burns's office. Mr. Burns was less understanding than he'd been before. He looked even taller than last time, too.

Mr. Burns stared down at Sean as he asked, "Someone has infected the computers in our media center with a virus. The computers shut down exactly three minutes after they're turned on. What do you know about this?"

"Nothing," Sean said. He squirmed. "Well, that is, I mean almost nothing. Maybe nothing."

Mr. Burns kept staring, so Sean tried to explain. "Yesterday, at home, I got an anonymous E-mail message. It said that I'd been in trouble but that today, *you* were going to have problems."

"Did I just hear you say that the E-mail message was anonymous?"

"Yes, sir."

"I'm sure that's impossible," Mr. Burns said. "Everyone who accesses the Internet has some kind of identifying name. In America Online it's a screen name. In Prodigy it's an I.D. code. I know that E-mail can't be sent anonymously."

"But it can," Sean said. "Brian said that—"

Mr. Burns interrupted. "Your brother, Brian, is a member of the junior high's computer club. No doubt he's aware of many computer tricks that can be played. He might very well be playing a trick on you with all this talk about anonymous E-mail. Maybe I should have a talk with him, too."

"No!" Sean said. "None of this is Brian's fault."

"We'll see about that," Mr. Burns said. "Even

though no one claims to have put the virus into the computers, I hold the computer club members either directly or indirectly responsible. Their sponsor has agreed that during their weekly visit to our school—which happens to be tomorrow—they'll try to find the virus in the computers and remove it. We might get some answers then."

The bell rang, and Mr. Burns asked, "For the record, tell me, Sean. Did you or your friends have anything to do with the computer virus?"

"No," Sean said. "We didn't."

Mr. Burns sighed. "Then you may be excused."

Sean looked up—way up—at Mr. Burns, who had a very tired expression on his face. "I'll tell you what, Mr. Burns," Sean said. "I promise that Bri and I will find out who put the virus in your computers."

"Maybe it would be better if we *didn't* have your help," Mr. Burns suggested, but Sean smiled encouragingly.

"Bri and I solve lots of crimes. We're the Casebusters. Just relax, Mr. Burns. We'll find out who did this."

Sean left the office to find Larry, Jabez, Debbie Jean, and a few other kids from his class waiting for him.

"What happened?" Jabez asked.

"Are you in trouble again?" Alison asked, glancing at Debbie Jean. "Is it about what you did with the computers yesterday?"

"I hope so," Debbie Jean said.

Sean noticed that the office door was open, and Mr. Burns could hear what he said. And Sean remembered what he had been told to do.

He squeezed his eyes shut and blurted out,

"Debbie Jean, I'm sorry I played that computer trick on you yesterday. I apologize."

Debbie Jean began to choke and cough. As she bent over, Alison slapped her hard on the back. A wad of chewing gum shot out of Debbie Jean's mouth.

Debbie Jean stood up and stared at Sean. "You shouldn't have done that," she complained.

"Done what? All I did was apologize."

"I know, but I wasn't expecting it. You surprised me, and that made me swallow my gum, and I nearly choked."

"You'd better pick up your gum," Larry said, "or you're going to step in it."

Debbie Jean scraped her wad of gum from the floor and made a face. "Oh, yuck!" she said. "Now it's got fuzz on it."

Charlie Miyako walked up to Sean, an

unhappy look on his face. "I told Mrs. Harrison that the magic computer was going to give me three wishes," he said. "But she said there was no magic computer. She said that somebody was playing a trick on me."

Sean couldn't stand to see Charlie look so miserable. "Don't give up," Sean said. "Just stop talking to everybody about magic computers. Keep your wishes secret, and maybe they'll start to come true."

"When?" Charlie asked.

"Like maybe starting tonight," Sean said. "Who knows?"

Charlie grinned as he ran off to his classroom.

Larry laughed as Debbie Jean complained, "You gave Charlie three wishes? You didn't give them to *me*."

As Sean walked to his fourth grade class he

asked himself, Why don't I think before I make promises? A giant candy bar is one thing, but there's no way I can come up with a new bike and a monster under Sam's bed.

* * *

IT WASN'T UNTIL they were leaving school that Sean was able to talk to Matt. At least, he *would* have talked to Matt, if Larry hadn't been so busy filling Matt in on everything that had happened that day.

As they pulled their bikes from the rack Larry said, "Mr. Burns thinks that you and Sean gave the computers a virus."

"No way," Matt managed to mumble. His face was puffy and numb with the anesthetic the dentist had given him.

"That's what I told Mr. Burns," Sean said as he hopped on his bike. "He kinda acted like he believed me, but I don't think he really does. He's blaming the kids in the junior high computer club, too, and that's not fair."

Just as the boys reached the street where they would part company, Larry's older brother Frank rode up on his bike. "C'mon, Larry," Frank said. "Mom said you're supposed to stop dawdling and come straight home."

"I'm not dawdling," Larry complained.

"Just get on home," Frank told him. Without saying a word to Matt or Sean, Frank took off. Larry pedaled hard to keep up.

"Sometimes I'm glad I don't have a big brother," Matt said. "Frank's a pain."

"Yeah," Sean said. Loyally, he added, "But Bri's okay—most of the time."

"Frank never speaks to us; it's as if we were invisible."

"Forget Frank," Sean said. "I have to ask you something. Have you gotten any anonymous E-mail letters?"

Matt stopped his bike. "What are you talking about? I've never even heard of an anonymous E-mail letter. You're kidding, right?"

Sean circled his bike before he stopped next to Matt. It gave him time to think. It might be better not to tell Matt about the anonymous letter. He didn't want everyone at school to know about it. "Just wondering," he said. "I'm cutting off here. I'm going to the store to get Charlie his giant candy bar."

Matt reached into his pocket for some change. "I'll go halves with you on the candy bar, but count me out on the bike."

"Thanks," Sean said. He rode off toward the store.

Later, when he arrived home, all Sean could think about was the computer and what he might find on it. Mom was still at work and

Brian was at basketball practice. If he turned on the computer to check for E-mail, he'd have to face any anonymous messages alone.

Sean went into his dad's office and stared at the computer. The blank, dark screen seemed to stare back, daring him to come nearer, taunting him to turn on the computer.

"I can do it," Sean said aloud. "I'm not some scared little kid."

He booted up the computer and got the message for mail. Sean clicked on the icon, and up came another E-mail, addressed to him: YOU'RE GIVING AWAY THREE WISHES? YOU SHOULD SAVE ONE FOR YOURSELF. I BET I CAN MAKE YOU WISH YOU NEVER HEARD OF COMPUTERS.

5

As soon as Brian came home, Sean showed him the message.

"Don't be scared," Brian said.

"Scared? Who's scared?" Sean said. He calmed down, then added, "Well, yeah. I guess I am—a little bit."

Brian clapped Sean on the shoulder. "This is turning out to be a mystery for the Casebusters to solve. We'll find out who's doing this."

Sean nodded. "I'm glad you think so. Today I promised Mr. Burns we'd solve the mystery of who put a virus into our school's computers."

"I heard about that," Brian said. "Mr. Burns seems to think our computer club's responsible, doesn't he?"

"Dennis Taylor is always bragging about pulling some kind of trick. Maybe Dennis put in the virus."

"I don't think so," Brian said. "Look, we've already figured out that the message is not only from someone who knows a lot about computers, but who also knows what's going on at your school. The only time Dennis is at your school is when our computer club comes to visit."

Sean jumped up. "Hey! I bet it's Sam! He's in the computer club. If Charlie told him about the three wishes trick Matt and I pulled, Sam might be playing a trick on us in turn."

"I don't know—" Brian began, but Sean interrupted.

"Sam's always telling scary stories. These

computer warnings are just the kind of thing he might pull."

"Okay," Brian said. He pulled out his notebook and began writing.

"What are you doing?" Sean asked.

"Making a list of possible suspects," Brian said. "We'll start with Sam." He tucked the notebook and pencil back into the pocket of his jeans and asked, "Why don't we talk to Sam right now?"

Brian and Sean went next door to the Miyakos' house.

As Sam invited them in, he leaned over and said to Sean, "It's a good thing you're here. I can warn you about the python."

"What python?" Sean asked.

"I heard it on the TV news," Sam said. He made his voice low and scary as he went on. "A large, dangerous python escaped from a zoo and can't be found. Pythons like to wrap themselves around their victims and squeeze them to death—maybe while they're sleeping."

"Yikes!" Sean said and shivered.

"Cut it out, Sam," Brian said. "That story was in the newspaper this morning, and the zoo's someplace far away in South America."

Sam shrugged. "You just ruined a perfectly good story," he said. "Sean started looking almost as scared as Charlie was when I told it to him."

"Poor Charlie," Sean said, glad that Bri was his big brother and not Sam.

"Let's talk about computers," Brian told Sam.

"Computers? That reminds me. Charlie told me some weird thing about a magic computer that's going to grant him three wishes."

Sean touched the giant chocolate bar under his shirt. "Where is Charlie?" he asked.

"He went to the store with Dad. He's been

bugging him for a new bike."

Sean jumped. "Wow! They went to buy Charlie a new bike?"

"No. They only went to the grocery store, but Charlie never gives up."

"Sit down," Brian told Sam. "I want to talk about what happened to the computers at Redoaks Elementary."

"Yeah, the virus," Sam said. "I wonder—"

Sean slipped out of the room and down to Charlie's bedroom. He tucked the chocolate bar under the bedspread on top of Charlie's pillow. Charlie would be sure to find it when he went to bed.

"Wish number one taken care of," Sean said happily. "Now it's time to get to work on wish number two." He walked to the kitchen to talk to Mrs. Miyako, who was setting the table for dinner.

"Hi, Mrs. Miyako," he said.

"Hi, Sean," Mrs. Miyako answered with a big smile.

"Is Charlie going to have a birthday soon?" Sean asked.

"Not for another six months," she said. "Why?"

"I was just thinking how nice it would be if Charlie got a new bike," Sean said.

Mrs. Miyako looked startled. "Charlie's been begging for a bigger bike," she said, "but my husband and I think that his old one has another good year in it."

"Aw, the poor guy," Sean said and tried to look sad. "There's nothing more embarrassing than riding around on a bike that's too small. He wants a new bike so badly. He even thinks a magic computer will make one appear."

"Oh, yes. We've heard about the magic

computer. What's that all about?"

"You might say that the magic computer is something like the tooth fairy," Sean said. "It's kind of for bigger kids, who've outgrown things like little kid bikes."

Mrs. Miyako frowned. "Hmmm. Maybe this is something my husband and I should think over. I'm glad you told me this, Sean."

"Glad to be of help," Sean said. "I'll see you later."

As he walked toward the living room where Brian and Sam were talking, Sean thought about the third wish—a monster under Sam's bed. He and Matt would have to give that one an awful lot of thought. Sean almost wished that the lost python wasn't so far away.

6

THE NEXT AFTERNOON the kids in the junior high computer club arrived at Redoaks Elementary. They immediately went to the media center and got busy trying to find the computer virus.

At first Sean couldn't find Brian. Then he saw him hanging over the shoulder of a dark-haired girl named Valerie Kincaid. Valerie and Brian were smiling at each other. Sean knew Valerie, and he'd seen her work with the computers. She was pretty good.

Sean walked up behind Brian and said, "Hi, Valerie. Hi, Bri. Bri, are you taking notes?"

"Go away," Brian mumbled.

"But you said—"

Brian reached into the pocket of his jeans and pulled out his notebook and pencil. He shoved it at Sean. "Here," he said. "You take notes." Brian went back to smiling at Valerie.

Sean stationed himself at the open door of the media center, where he could watch all the members of the computer club. At the top of the page he wrote down Valerie's name. A few spaces below it he wrote, DENNIS TAYLOR.

Dennis liked to play tricks, and it would have been easy for him to do something weird with the computers.

Some of the kids in the computer club were cracking jokes. Some were trying to give orders to the computers and saying, "Ooops!" when the computers didn't respond. But Neal York was really concentrating on his computer, his hands tapping rapidly on the keyboard. Neal was one of the best in the computer club. Neal would have known how to put the virus into the computers, Sean thought.

A voice whispered in Sean's ear. "What are you doing?"

Sean jumped and whirled around to see Debbie Jean. "I'm taking notes," he said.

Debbie Jean looked excited. "You're on a case?"

Sean winced. "Keep it down. Mrs. Harrison and Mr. Burns think I'm the one messing everything up. Bri and I just want to find out who's really causing the trouble."

Debbie Jean glanced at Brian, who seemed to be more interested in Valerie than in the computer in front of them. "Brian's on the case? Oh, sure," she said.

"Quiet. Right now he's hot on the trail of a

suspect, so he's undercover," Sean told her.

Larry and Matt suddenly crowded in behind Debbie Jean. "What's going on?" Larry asked.

"The Casebusters are on a job," Debbie Jean told them. "They're going to find out who messed up the computers."

"Be quiet!" Sean said.

He watched the computer club students and wrote down the rest of their names.

Suddenly Neal looked up and said, "No more virus, Mrs. Harrison. I found it."

Mrs. Harrison leaned over Neal's shoulder to look at the monitor in front of him.

"The virus was just a timing device," Neal explained. "The computers were set to operate correctly again when the timing device shut itself off on Friday. I just shut it down early."

"I'm so glad you found the virus!" Mrs. Harrison exclaimed. "It would have been terrible to be without our computers for the rest of the week."

"No problem," Neal said. "This wasn't a really great virus. I remember when Frank Grier found a virus that took six hours to fix."

"Frank's good," Valerie said. "It's too bad he can't be in our computer club."

"He can join next semester," Brian told her. "He said he wants to as soon as the school lets him."

Neal stood up and gave a friendly pat to the monitor. "You won't have any more trouble with this virus, Mrs. Harrison," he said. "It's gone now. This one was almost too simple. Any kid who knows computers could have put this virus in."

"Oh, really?" Mrs. Harrison said. As she stepped back she turned and saw Sean in the doorway.

"Sean Quinn, I'm going to take you off computers for a week," she said. "That goes for Matt, too."

"But we—"

"Just get along to class," she said. "Mrs. Jackson wouldn't want you to loiter down here."

"I don't loiter," Sean mumbled to himself. As he turned to leave the media center, he said to his friends, "You see? Everybody's blaming Matt and me for something we didn't do."

Sean had barely left the doorway when Charlie nearly slammed into him. "Mrs. Harrison!" Charlie yelled, rushing into the media center. "The first wish came true! I got my candy bar!"

He ran to the computer he thought was magic and hugged it. Then he dashed past

Sean, shouting, "You were right! I believed my wish would come true, and it did!"

Sean grinned, but Debbie Jean scowled at him. "He got his first wish from the magic computer?"

"Yeah," Sean said, "A giant chocolate bar."

"Huh," Debbie Jean said. "If that's what the computer is handing out, then I'd like one, too."

"Sorry," Sean said. "You'll have to connect with the magic computer to get your wishes. I haven't got anything to do with it—especially when I can't even get near the computers for a week."

* * *

AFTER SCHOOL BRIAN and Sean rode their bikes home, but they didn't talk much. It wasn't until they were inside their house, fortified with cookies and milk, that Brian said,

"Don't feel bad about what Mrs. Harrison told you. I explained that you and Matt had nothing to do with the computer virus and that you and I were trying to solve the case."

"She believed you? Honestly?" Sean asked.

"Well, not exactly," Brian said. "I think she's going to need more proof."

"Like finding out who really did it," Sean said.

"Right," Brian said. "But she told me to tell you she's sorry she acted so hastily and she'd like you to come and talk with her."

Maybe she'd let him come back to the media center, Sean hoped. He hated to be away from it for a whole long week. "I wrote down the names of everybody in the computer club, starting with Valerie," Sean said and handed Brian his notebook and pencil. "What do we do next?"

"What we always do with any case," Brian said. "We'll gather evidence. Let's start by seeing if you've got any new E-mail."

"I don't think I want to find out," Sean mumbled. But he soon found himself eagerly leaning over Brian's shoulder as the E-mail appeared.

The E-mail letter read: I'M GLAD YOU'RE THE ONE IN TROUBLE. YOU INTERFERING QUINNS LIKE GETTING EVERYONE ELSE IN TROUBLE. NOW IT'S YOUR TURN.

"Yikes!" Sean said.

Brian looked pleased. "Now we have a clue," he said. "A very important clue that could tell us who this is."

7

SEAN STARED AT the message on the monitor's screen. "What clue?" he asked. "What are you talking about?"

"Now we know it's someone the Casebusters got in trouble. Or maybe it's a criminal from one of Dad's cases."

"Would this criminal be mad at you and me, too?"

"I don't know," Brian said. "Here's Dad's disk with reports of cases he's solved."

He inserted the disk into the computer and brought up the contents. "Let's see if this tells us anything," he said. He used the FIND key and typed in: COMPUTER. "We have to remember that whoever put the virus into your school's computers knows a lot about computers."

"And knows everything going on at my school," Sean added.

Brian suddenly gulped and leaned back from the computer.

Sean bent over him, trying to read the screen, but Brian put his hands in front of it.

"This was a bad idea. Let's forget it," Brian said.

"No. You found something. Let me see," Sean insisted.

Brian didn't move. "I think I should work on this clue by myself." he said.

"Why?" Sean asked. "I'm the one getting the E-mail. I'm the one being spied on."

Brian shrugged and moved away from the

computer so that Sean could read what was on the screen.

CLIENT: CYBER-DYNAMIC COMPUTER STORE

CASE: SHOPLIFTING

RESULT: ARREST OF PETER KINCAID BY REDOAKS POLICE. CASE CLOSED.

Sean straightened and looked at Brian. "What's the big deal? Who's Peter Kincaid?" he asked.

"Valerie's uncle," Brian said unhappily.

"Hey! Maybe Valerie's been sending that creepy E-mail because she's mad about her uncle being arrested," Sean said. He felt a little better because Valerie didn't look mean and scary. Then a thought occurred to him. "How does she know all the things that are going on at my school?"

"Maybe she finds out when she comes with the computer club to help in the media center."

"She wasn't there when I got in trouble the first time," Sean pointed out. "No one from the computer club was at school that day."

Brian sighed with relief. "You're right," he said. "It couldn't be Valerie."

"Who's doing this?" Sean asked. "Whoever it is knows all about everything that happens to me at school. How do they find out?"

Brian looked serious. "Even more important, what is our mystery person planning to do next?"

* * *

THE NEXT DAY, before school started, Sean paid a visit to Mrs. Harrison. "Brian said you wanted to see me," Sean said.

Mrs. Harrison nodded. "I was upset and I overreacted yesterday, Sean. I had no right to accuse you of tampering with the computers. I'm sorry."

"I didn't do it," Sean said, "but my brother Bri and I are going to find out who did."

Mrs. Harrison sighed. "It may be very difficult."

Sean nodded. "We'll do it anyway," he said. "No case is too tough for the Casebusters. We solve lots of crimes."

Mrs. Harrison gave a long sigh and looked tired. "You'll be careful of my media center, won't you?"

"Sure," Sean said. He tried to make her look happier by joking, "We hardly ever leave bodies or smashed-up computers lying around."

But Mrs. Harrison didn't laugh. "You'd better hurry on to class before the bell rings," she said.

"Okay," Sean said. "See you this afternoon when the computer club kids are here." As he walked to Mrs. Jackson's room, he wondered why Mrs. Harrison had looked even more unhappy.

* * *

DURING LUNCH PERIOD, Jabez teased Sean. "Hey, Sean, you haven't been sent to Mr. Burns's office all morning."

Matt spoke through a large mouthful of macaroni and cheese. "Yeah. Maybe that's a record," he said.

"Some friend *you* are." Sean elbowed Matt in the ribs. "The only reason you weren't in the principal's office with me was because you were at the dentist."

Larry stepped up to the table and plopped down his tray. "Did you hear the big news?" he asked. "They're going to put a special chair in the principal's office with Sean's name on it."

"A chair, too? Wow!" Jabez said. "I heard they're putting out a WELCOME SEAN mat in front of the office door."

Sean tried to be a good sport and pretend that he thought the teasing was funny, but he didn't. From the corners of his eyes he glanced around the room. The cafeteria was filled with busy people. None of them looked as though they were paying any attention to Sean, but he knew that someone must be secretly watching—the someone who seemed to know everything that Sean was doing.

That evening, wishing that Brian weren't at basketball practice again, Sean carefully closed the drapes in his dad's office. When he was positive that no one could look in and see him, he booted up the computer and checked the E-mail.

"Yikes!" he cried. There was another E-mail letter addressed to him. Did he want to read it? Or should he wait until Brian came home?

Sean's fingers shook as he clicked on the icon, and the letter appeared on the screen.

YOU'RE BEING TEASED, AND YOU DON'T LIKE IT. ALL THE KIDS TEASED ME WHEN I WENT TO REDOAKS ELEMENTARY, TOO. NOW IT'S MY TURN TO HAVE SOME FUN. I'M GOING TO GET EVEN.

"Another clue!" Sean told Brian as soon as Brian had come home and read the message.

"It's not much of a clue," Brian answered.

"Sure, it is," Sean said. "First, we find out how many kids in the computer club went to Redoaks Elementary."

"I can tell you that," Brian said. "All of them."

"Uh-oh," Sean said, but he soon perked up. "Okay, then. We find out which ones got teased in school."

"It won't work," Brian said.

Sean shook his head. "You're wrong, Bri."

"No, I'm not."

"You are, too," Sean insisted. "Watch me. I'm going to prove it."

8

THE NEXT AFTERNOON, when it came time for the junior high computer club to work with the Redoaks Elementary kids in the media center, Sean planned to station himself in the hallway, just outside the door.

But Mrs. Jackson kept the class a few minutes too long, and Sean was late. Most of his class and the kids from Redoaks Junior High were in the center, but Neal York arrived a few minutes late. Sean stepped in front of him.

"Hi, Neal," Sean said. "I'm taking a poll.

Were you teased when you went to school here at Redoaks Elementary?"

"Sure, I was," Neal said. "I always got good grades, so some kids teased me about being a nerd."

"Did the teasing make you mad?"

"I guess it bothered me when I was younger," Neal said. "But not anymore."

Valerie and Brian were so busy talking as they came to the media center, they didn't see Sean.

"Wait, Valerie," Sean said. He jumped out in front of them. "I have a question for you." He didn't care that he was interrupting. This was detective work, wasn't it? He didn't give Valerie or Brian time to object. "Were you teased when you went here to school?"

Valerie looked surprised, then she giggled. "Some of the kids used to tease me about my name. They called me 'Valerie-celery,' and I hated it."

"You hated it, hmmm?" Sean said. He decided that no matter how much Brian liked Valerie, she was still on the list of suspects.

"You go on, Valerie," Brian said. "I'll catch up with you." As soon as Valerie was out of hearing range, Brian said to Sean, "I told you, you won't get any information this way. Everybody gets teased in elementary school."

Not giving Sean a chance to interrupt, Brian went on. "Dennis was always losing things, and he got teased so much he decided to say funny things before anyone else could. That's why he makes jokes all the time. Frank and Neal were teased about being nerds because they studied a lot, and for a while the kids called Sam 'Sammy-Hammy' when they wanted to make him mad."

"What did the kids tease you about, Bri?" Sean asked.

Brian looked at his watch and said, "I'm late. I have to go help in the computer lab." He hurried inside without answering the question.

Sean managed to ask most of the kids in the computer club about being teased, but all it added up to was the same old stuff. They were teased about being overweight or underweight, running slowly or striking out, having freckles, big ears, or girlfriends. None of them were reasons for getting mad at the Quinns or playing tricks with the school's computers.

Sean was discouraged as he and Brian rode their bikes home from school.

As soon as they were in the house, Brian said, "Let's check the computer for more E-mail."

But Sean threw his backpack on a chair. "Who cares?" he said. "I don't want anything else to do with the mystery mailer who's spying on me."

"Aw, c'mon, Sean," Brian coaxed. "He's been sloppy with his clues. This time he may give himself away."

Just as Brian had suspected, there was an E-mail letter for Sean. Brian brought it up, and both he and Sean leaned close to the monitor to read what it had to say:

YOU CAN'T FOOL ME. I KNOW YOU'RE ASKING QUESTIONS AND TRYING TO FIND ME. BACK OFF, OR YOU'LL REALLY BE IN TROUBLE.

Sean sat down with a thump. "Another threat," he said.

"Hey, don't look so worried," Brian said. "I'm going to check some other disks Dad uses. We ought to be able to come up with names of kids—not grownups—who might have been in trouble."

It didn't take long to discover that there weren't any names of kids on the disks. "It's probably because all juvenile records are sealed. Sorry," Brian said.

He put a hand on Sean's shoulder and smiled. "Tell you what, tomorrow's Friday. After school I'll take you to the mall and we'll go through Monstermadness. Forget the computer nut who's been bugging us. We're going to have fun."

"Great!" Sean said and grinned at Brian. He quickly turned off the computer. But it wasn't as easy to turn off all the questions he had in mind. Someone had got him in trouble. Someone had scared him. And now someone was after him.

Who? Sean thought. Who are you?

9

EVERYTHING WAS IN confusion Friday morning, as Sean arrived at school. People were hurrying up and down the stairs and through the halls. The bells rang. There was a short pause, and they rang again.

"What's going on?" Sean yelled at Debbie Jean.

She opened her mouth and said something, but at the same time the bells rang two shorts and a long, making it hard to hear.

"What?"

It was suddenly silent. Debbie Jean said again, "The bells are going crazy. Well, not the bells, exactly. The computer that times and rings the bells is crazy."

The bells rang again—a long bell that went on and on. Sean scrunched up his face and clapped his hands over his ears.

In the sudden silence that followed, a stern voice came over the intercom: "Will Sean Quinn please report immediately to the principal's office?"

Sean groaned. "Oh, not again."

As soon as he entered the principal's office, Sean protested, "I didn't have anything to do with the bells!"

"The bells are timed on the school's main computer system," Mr. Burns said.

Sean wondered if Mr. Burns had grown six inches since he last saw him. "But I didn't change the computer," Sean said. "I don't even know how it's done."

"We'll discuss this later. Right now, I want you to turn those bells off."

Sean looked way, way up and said, "I told you, Mr. Burns, I don't know how to."

Mr. Burns frowned as he thought—and as he grew another inch or two. "Hmmm," he said. "Our custodian can probably disconnect the electrical system until whoever knows how to reset the system can get here. I'll call the main office."

Mr. Burns didn't actually excuse Sean to go to class, but he became so busy making phone calls that Sean left the office. He was sure that Mr. Burns didn't believe him, and he felt bad about it. On Sean's way to his class the bells rang just once, then stopped.

Sean was the last of his class to arrive in the room.

"Good morning, Sean," Mrs. Jackson said.

"Good morning, Mrs. Jackson," Sean said.

"I didn't do it."

"Cheer up," she said. "I believe you." She smiled and added, "I heard that Brian made Top Student of the Month. Congratulate him for me."

Sean perked up, glad that he could brag about Bri with the whole class listening. "He got some cool prizes," Sean said. "Including two free Monstermadness games at the arcade in the mall. We're going to Monstermadness right after school."

"Lucky!" Matt said. "I love Monstermadness."

"Yeah. I wish my brother Frank had won," Larry said. "We all thought he had a chance at winning, because he really worked on his grades, and he helped with the recycling drive."

"Well, I think Monstermadness is stupid," Debbie Jean said. "All you do is wander around in pitch black tunnels, shooting laser lights at weird faces that pop out of the wall. Is that dumb or what?"

The whole class began arguing, until Mrs. Jackson called for order and began their history lesson.

Later, after school, Sean told Brian what had happened. "Mr. Burns still thinks I'm causing all the trouble," he complained.

He expected Brian to worry, too, but instead Brian grinned. "This is great," he said. "We just got another important clue. Not everyone would know how to get to the main computer."

"But how would we find out who—"

"The person in the computer club who knows the most about computers is Neal," Brian explained. "Let's investigate him."

"But Monstermadness . . ."

"We'll have time for that, too," Brian said. "Grab your bike. I know where Neal's family lives. Let's go."

When the door opened at the Yorks' apartment, Brian and Sean found that Dennis Taylor was visiting Neal. Brian told them what had happened at Redoaks Elementary, and Dennis laughed.

"What a great joke," he said. "If I'd been there, I would have read the poem 'The Bells,' by Edgar Allan Poe."

Neal rubbed his chin. "Let's see," he said. "Someone would have to know that the bells were set by computer and know how to get into the computer."

"How about you?" Brian asked. "Did you know?"

"I thought Edgar Allan Poe only wrote scary stories," Sean said.

"What do you mean, did I know?" Neal asked Brian.

"Poe wrote lots of poems, too," Dennis said.

"Everybody hold it!" Brian said. "Forget Edgar Allan Poe. We're trying to find out what happened at Sean's school. The principal's blaming him."

"I thought you might be blaming me," Neal said. "Our family doesn't even own a computer."

"Then how did you get to be one of the best in our computer club?" Brian asked.

Neal shrugged. "They let me use the computers at school," he said.

"I kind of like the idea of bells ringing all day," Dennis said. "Neal, could you program the computer at our junior high to do that?"

"No way," Neal said. "I mean I could, but I don't want to get into trouble and be kicked out of the computer club, like Frank was."

"Frank'll be okay," Dennis said. "He's been

doing everything just right so he won't get into trouble again."

"How could Frank get in trouble so fast?" Sean asked. "Isn't this his first year in junior high?"

"He got into trouble while he was still in Redoaks Elementary," Brian explained.

"Brian's the one who discovered what was going on," Dennis told Sean. "Brian noticed that one of the student computer accounts on the Internet was busy, even though the student had moved away. When he told Mrs. Harrison, she found out that Frank was using the account."

"What's the big deal about using somebody else's account?" Sean asked. "And why would he, when he had an account of his own?"

"Account time is limited," Brian said. "Kids who use others' accounts get double time on the Internet. Besides, they're supposed to be using the accounts for research and study, and sometimes they use the extra account to play games and stuff. You know the rules. They're not supposed to do that."

Neal yawned. "Let's talk about something else," he said. "Anybody want some leftover pizza?"

"No thanks," Brian said. "I have a couple more questions I need to ask you, Neal."

"Later," Neal said. "This is Friday. I don't want to think any more about school. Anybody want a soda?"

"Some other time," Brian said. "Sean and I are going to the mall to play Monstermadness."

Dennis grinned. "It's awfully dark and scary in there. Don't let the monsters get you! You might never be seen again!"

10

A SHORT WHILE LATER, as they waited in line for their turn at Monstermadness, Sean asked Brian, "Neal didn't want to answer our questions. Do you know why?"

Brian shrugged. "He's high on our list of suspects. Neal knows so much about computers, he'd know how to arrange for an anonymous mailer. And he'd know how to make the school's bells ring all day long."

"But how would Neal know everything that happens to me at school?" Sean asked.

Brian shrugged. "Beats me."

The ticket taker working at Monstermadness called to Brian and Sean, "Step up, guys. It's your turn." He handed Sean something called a *super lightray* and asked, "Have you done this before?"

"Yes," Brian said.

"No," Sean said.

"Okay. You go first," the ticket taker said to Sean. "Here are the rules. Only one person can go into Monstermadness at a time. As you walk through the tunnels, monster faces will pop out at you. You get points for every monster you hit with your lightray."

"Cool!" Sean said. He could hardly wait to start.

"Just remember, the tunnels twist around and are really dark, and the monsters pop up fast," Brian reminded Sean.

Clutching his lightray, Sean entered

Monstermadness. As the door closed behind him and everything became dark, he felt a little nervous.

A scary monster face suddenly appeared on Sean's right side. He aimed his lightray at it and pulled the trigger. A sign flashed, 25 POINTS.

Sean began to walk forward, watching for monsters. Another popped up so quickly that Sean jumped and missed it. Quickly came another and another. Sean didn't know which side to look at first. He shot wildly and missed.

Suddenly a voice behind Sean whispered in his ear. "Back off trying to find me, or I'll give you more trouble than you can handle."

"Yikes!" Sean screeched.

Someone brushed against him, but he couldn't see anything in the dark. Monster faces flashed and disappeared, but Sean's knees wobbled and his hands shook. He was much too scared to move.

"Bri!" he managed to squeak, but he knew Brian couldn't hear him and wouldn't come.

"I've got to get out of here!" Sean cried out. He ran forward and bounced into a wall. He turned and hit another wall. Close to panic he struggled into the last tunnel.

When he finally saw a thin line of light under the exit doorway, he let out a yelp and ran for it. Slamming through the swinging exit door, Sean ran out into the mall.

"Bri?" he called. But Brian was nowhere in sight.

Sean yelled to the ticket taker, "Where's my brother?"

"I sent him into the maze when you were halfway through," the ticket taker said. He reached for Sean's super lightray and laughed.

"What happened to you? You only got a score of twenty-five. Did you freak out?"

"Someone was in there with me," Sean grumbled.

"Sure. I told you. Your brother." The ticket taker pointed to an electronic scoreboard. "There's his score up there. You can see he's started out pretty well."

Inside Monstermadness, Brian racked up lots of points, because he carefully watched for monsters. Alert, he caught a slight motion off to one side and called out, "Sean? Are you still in here?"

No one answered, so Brian swung his lightray to the right and caught a glimpse of a figure dressed in black.

The figure ducked his head, dove out of the beam of the lightray, and disappeared.

For a few moments Brian tried to find the

mysterious person, but whoever had been there had left.

Disgusted at all the points he'd missed, Brian exited the tunnel.

Sean ran up to him. "Someone was in the tunnel with me, Bri!" he said.

The ticket taker glanced at the scoreboard and smiled at Brian. "You started out well," he said. "What happened? Did you get scared, too?"

"Somebody was in there," Brian complained.

"Look, like I told your brother, I don't let anyone in except the people playing the game. Okay? If you don't like your scores and want to play again, then you have to pay."

"Let's go, Bri," Sean said. "I've got something important to tell you."

As they climbed on their bikes Sean told

Brian what the person in black had said.

"Who knew we were coming here?" Brian asked. "I only told Neal and Dennis. Oh, yeah, Sam, too."

"Uh-oh," Sean said. "Mrs. Jackson was bragging about your being Top Student of the Month, and I told my whole class that we were going to Monstermadness after school."

"The kids in your class wouldn't know enough about computers to write an anonymous mailer or make the school's bells ring."

"But they could have told someone else," Sean insisted. His bike wobbled as he drove along the edge of a pothole, but he balanced it and caught up to Brian. "Why do you think the mystery person has to be a member of the computer club?"

"Detectives deal in facts, so let's look at the facts," Brian answered. "There are three things we know about the person who sends the mysterious messages. They're good with computers, they know what's going on at your school, and they blame the Quinns for getting them into trouble."

As they arrived home, Brian and Sean dropped their bikes and helmets on the grass. Sean pulled a sheet of paper from his pocket. "Sam Miyako's out as a suspect. He's never been in trouble," Sean said. "Dennis Taylor and Neal York we don't know about. So that leaves Valerie Kincaid, whose uncle got in trouble on account of Dad's investigation."

A loud shout made Sean jump. He turned to see Charlie leap off his front porch and run toward him.

"Sean!" Charlie yelled. "The magic computer gave me the first wish! Now the second is coming true! Mom and Dad decided to get me a bigger bike!"

"Cool," Sean said.

"What's your third wish?" Brian asked Charlie.

"I can't tell my wishes until after they come true," Charlie answered. "You can't talk about secrets."

Charlie ran home, and Brian asked Sean, "Does Charlie's magic computer and all that three wishes stuff have anything to do with you and Matt and your computer tricks?"

"Bri," Sean said slowly. "I think Charlie just gave us the answer. There's a suspect we haven't talked about, and I think we can catch him if we set a trap."

11

IMPATIENTLY, SEAN WAITED until Sunday. Then he telephoned Larry—supposedly to check on a homework assignment. "My dad's coming home today," Sean said. "That means I won't have the chance to use the computer for a while. I'll have to check my account at school to see if I get any E-mail."

After Sean and Larry ended their conversation, Sean asked Brian, "Will it work?"

"I hope so," Brian said.

Sean sighed. "If it doesn't, I'll be in a lot more trouble at school than I am now."

Like one of Charlie's secrets, Sean tried not to think about the plan he and Brian had worked out. So it wasn't until Monday, after school, that Sean checked for E-mail under his school account in the Redoaks Elementary media center.

Exactly as he had expected, there was an anonymous mailer, taunting him for not being able to use his computer at home. Mr. Burns and Mrs. Harrison, who had been told about the plan, stood behind Sean and Brian, reading the message on the screen.

"You were right, Sean," Brian said. "The person causing the computer problems is Frank. He got the information about you from his brother Larry."

"I'm sorry for doubting you, Sean," Mrs. Harrison said, "but after the tricks you and Matt played . . . well, you can see why I was suspicious, can't you?"

Mr. Burns said, "I'll make a phone call to Frank Grier's parents. We'll soon have this problem taken care of." He cleared his throat and added, "Thank you, Sean and Brian, for solving the case."

"The Casebusters did it again," Brian said, "with nothing to work on but bare facts."

"Bare facts?" Sean said. "Hmmm. That gives me another idea."

* * *

THAT EVENING SEAN and Matt struggled to put the finishing touches on a gruesome thing made out of a stuffed shirt and pants. At the end of its arms were pinned the bear paw slippers, and its pillowcase head was covered with a weird Halloween mask and wig.

"This is hard work," Matt complained.

"Don't blame me," Sean said. "You were the magic computer handing out three wishes.

When we're ready, Brian's going to keep Sam and Charlie out of the way, and Mrs. Miyako is going to let us in the back door so we can put this under Sam's bed."

"What if Sam doesn't look under his bed? He might never find it."

Sean grinned. "I'm going to tie a thread from one of the bear paws to the corner of Sam's blanket. When he throws back the covers to get into bed, the paw will reach out and hit his leg."

Within a half hour, the monster was in place.

Sean went to bed at his regular bedtime, but couldn't get to sleep. Would the monster work? Would it really scare Sam? Would Charlie be happy that his third wish had come true?

Still awake at 10:30, Sean heard a horrible yell coming from the Miyakos' house. Their lights flipped on, and he could hear Charlie shrieking with laughter.

Sean rolled over and contentedly closed his eyes. You can always count on the Casebusters, he thought. When we take a case, we never fail to tie up all the loose ends.

Joan Lowery Nixon is a renowned writer of children's mysteries. She is the author of more than eighty books and the only four-time recipient of the prestigious Edgar Allan Poe Award for the best juvenile mystery of the year.

☾

"I was asked by Disney Adventures *magazine if I could write a short mystery. I decided to write about two young boys who help their father, a private investigator, solve crimes. These boys, Brian and Sean, are actually based on my grandchildren, who are the same ages as the characters. My first Casebusters story was a piece about a ghost that haunts an inn. This derives from a legendary Louisiana inn I visited, which was allegedly haunted. Later, I learned the owner had made up the entire tale, and I used that angle in the story."*

— *Joan Lowery Nixon*